MIRAGASIA

Journal of Ewl

The Uprising

M. A. FENECH

INFINITY
BOOKS

Published by Infinity Books Ltd, Malta

www.infinitybooksmalta.com

Copyright © 2020 Maryanne Fenech and Infinity Books

ISBN: 9798569867288

Proofreading and editing by André Zahra

Ccover illustration by Lynn Zammit Russell.

AN INK-SPLOTCH TWISTED, AND SO DID MIRAGASIA

DIURNAL I

The multicoloured quill in my hand has a will of its own. I am using it to write with, it has a delicate feel and writes neatly. I'm using the few empty pages of my beloved journal. Or perhaps it would be more accurate to say the journal I despise so much...

Untarnishable ink fills my life, with a novel concept to eke out my miserable durnals. Perhaps writing is the key. I had always believed it was paintings, or creating a book of incantations. Which, I need to add I have not worked on in some time, and I think I will discard it. It did not help at all.

I am peckish, I always am. I do hope that who reads this journal will understand me, as I am not good with spelling and grammar... Godmother constantly scolds me for that. And not only for that, though I will do my utmost to write clearly. I am not only peckish but also impetuous, and obstinate. Godmother's words, and at times Martynn's and Toyol's.

I am writing this piece in the quietness and remoteness of my bed-chamber, with a grumbling stomach, in the castle where I have lived with my Godmother since I was born. That was sixteen aniums ago. Toyol lives with us, too, she is a crony. She is the cook. She taught me how to cook. Because I love eating, I cannot say that I love eating above everything else, because there are other things which I love more. I do not consider myself to be a gourmand but when it concerns gastronomy, I am quite a thinker and gluttony is my forte. More of an epicure as once my other crony, Martynn, called me. Well, in all honesty, I'm unsure whether or not to call him a crony, as he didn't really care about my well-being, or about being sincere with me about his private life. He kept many things hidden from me, especially about his son. This made me so livid when I got to know he has a son! So livid that I transformed or polymorphed, not sure. I never had that much of a flair for words! I just know I was livid – and I became a monster of wildfire! Not as wild as I wanted to spread. Well ... I want to burn Miragasia away. I want everyone to die! All apart from one – or two. I don't want Toyol to die, neither do I want Lenom to die – but Martynn and Vellià can go bury themselves alive! This wound you have is a spot which drops from the rheumy in my eyes. It will dry out... with time. I might ask Martynn about his son, and the reason for his falsehood in this aspect. Perhaps, he also was unsincere about other stuff. I tried asking Toyol, some durnals ago, she did not have an answer. She does not know Martynn as well as I thought she knew him. This irks me. I do not want to think about it anymore!

I am going to sleep.

This is how I surmise I transformed - A large creature, made of fire and coal, perhaps eight feet high, with wide wings, claws, and horns, and fangs which breathes flames, even from the eyes, which combusts at will. Only, I did not have the will! Irritatingly enough!

DIURNAL II

I surmise it is much better form of courtesy to date the durnals I wrote in, and keep track of how many durnals I started writing on this journal. So I will date every durnal I wrote in. And skip the ones I do not.

I had thought that the blank pages of this journal were meant to write about yourself, and then once you finish, something Seherial would happen. But it did not. Perhaps then it is just meant to write on ... perhaps there is some other way to make the Seher work. For now, it is just another means to rant out the misery in which I live. I do not know if it was meant for me to write on, Godmother said I can have it, after... after... oh! I got into so much trouble when she noticed I found it! Or wait! Irked I'm irked! When she decided I should be in trouble for finding it, she did reveal that it was intentional, she knew I had it or she knew I had you. We're not talking at present, as I am grounded for that whole transformation issue, and me running away, and getting to know the world, my grandfather, and finding you... all this lead to yet another unjust confinement. I do not know for how long. You and Wenilea are my only company. So I am going to write what comes to my mind.

Perhaps it has to do with the multicoloured quill Martynn presented to me... Perhaps writing with this quill will activate the Seher.

I am Ewliena...

Nothing... I live in a castle, with my godmother... correction — my gruesome godmother.

Bah! Nothing... not the quill either. Perhaps then I should change colour or writing style.

Let me try vibrant red.

I am Ewliena ...

This is frustrating; I know there is something Seherial to this journal!!

Come on. Work your magic!

DIURNAL III

One other form of courtesy when writing is to start each date on a new page. It should be the proper way of keeping documentation, Godmother would tell me to do that if she knew what I was doing. Perhaps she does, Wenilea did not see any other spies in my chamber, or so she told me. Wenilea is my gullinfern, Godmother helped me in creating her. It is a long process creating one, and a tad painful too... But in the end I found it to be rewarding.

I do not feel like writing about that here, I want to use these few remaining, empty pages to try to make sense of this seher.

Unified, unifying, uniformity... ... unf... unify... I want to unify the world, make peace with life...

Nothing, not even my most inner thoughts seem to ignite the Seher.

Instigate... instant, instigator... development... de...

Hrmph! Nothing!

Instigate... Why, I'm, I'm thinking about this word... the main instigator... initiate... organise, initiate; I am an initiate...

Activate Seher...

Actuate Seher... kindle...

I am Ewliena, I am Ewliena....

How many times do I have to write that I am Ewliena? I'm now exasperated! I have tried everything. Then it is set – you are just pieces of parchments bound together and meant to be written on. There is nothing more to you.

A thought struck me. I heard many a time mention of the magic of the written word and the legacy it lingers for generations to come. Perhaps, this is all about you, just my life for others to read as I have read the former owner's. Said text vanished from your pages the instant I started writing... Alas, really. It was a good text.

I am sleepy now... sweet dreams.

DIURNAL IIII

Let me then write how this multicoloured quill came to me, I want to tell someone, apart from Toyol, she already knows all about me and Martynn who has gifted me the quill...

That particular durnal had begun like every other one of mine —

wake up, wash, have breakfast, make my bed, and start my academic work. But that durnal, Xemxa was especially brilliant, it was scorching, and I wanted to go outside, to climb Makkja, and go for a ride with Donious – my hmejel. It so happened, that for some unexplainable reason, God-mother said yes. It happens so rarely. The happiness of that 'yes' got cut short, though – too good to last - with a: 'when you finish your studies!'

Bah! I so wanted to go outside, that I told her I had finished already – falsehood used to come so naturally to me at times. How I ever managed to be so glib about such a serious matter will always remain beyond my wits. But I had managed to deceive her at that time. I manipulated her in believing I really had. Or... well, as I so painfully understood, later on, she was the one who manipulated me. It was another ploy of hers.

I don't know why. But I had thought, I only have one history exercise to finish, how long can that take me? I can come back just in time to finish it off before dinner...

Astonishingly enough - it was too easy - she accepted my answer, with a 'you can go then, but remember the rules'. I should have understood that it was too good to last. But so great was my wish to get outdoors, that I managed to rid of the oddity, with a 'thank you,

Godmother,' and I skedaddled outside. How can I ever forget the rules? Finish your studies before dinner, then we would dine, and afterwards, she would look at the work I did – and find something to complain about. That was so methodic, that was the norm for me. Admittingly, I didn't put much of an effort into my so-called 'duties'. I hated them most of the time. Subsequently, I got myself to like them. What other choice did I have?

That's my life, but it's not the worst part...

Well, I had my fun on that durnal, until I heard the kitchen bell toll; it was Toyol ringing it, meaning it was time for me to head back inside. Fortunately, I had already put Donious back into his stall, so I headed inside. It was all peaceful, all as per routine, but I was not unmindful of the still-to-finish-work.

After much deliberation, I came up with the perfect stratagem: I had decided to lock myself in the lavatory room, faking a tummy-ache... (the lavatory chamber was a sanctuary of mine, especially when I was sick, I would not be disturbed there). Instead, I would be finishing off my academics, which I had all solidly written in my mind. It only needed inking...

Only, my plan got interrupted as soon as I entered the dining-chamber, where there was a surprise waiting for me... Martynn, I gasped. Not wanting to believe he was really there, his presence flabbergasted me (too much astonishment for one diurnal), made my heart miss a beat and flow undisturbed around my chest. It went pit-pat, pit-a-pat... pit.

Despite the perplexity I rushed to hug him – it had only happened one other time that he visits during dinner time. And he had dinner with us. I was so excited, I could hardly eat, but I did. With all the excitement I had forgotten all about the falsehood I previously mentioned and the stratagem to get out of it.

Until the usual command came, 'time to inspect your work'. My heart stopped then, completely. I had no other choice, but to confess and prepare for the worst. I drank of few restorative sips of Makkja's juice.

I was shaking whilst telling her, keeping my gaze away from Martynn, and my head low in submission.

I stood impatiently awaiting consequences.

Oddly enough, the only thing she said was 'go to your chamber.' That is all. I did not know what to think and had it not been for Martynn, who caught my wrist and dragged me out of the dining chamber, I would have frozen on the spot whilst eating away my insides. Such was my perplexity. If I had to give this recollection a title, I would definitely call it: The diurnal of bafflement.

Now, I have to add, with reluctance, that Godmother did make-up for the lack of scolding-punishment when Martynn left, and the diurnal after that and to a certain extent the following one too. According to Godmother, I am devious because I defied her, by trying to deceive her. Some tongue-twister.

And I understood that it had been Martynn and his presence which held her back, that time. It never happened again!

And now that I come to think of it, she knew all the way. It is obvious, her spies told her... She knew all along that I had lied - She was testing me... She gave me permission to get outside, to see for how long I would keep the act going. This saddens me, or angers me, or worse — but I'd rather not think about how my life makes me feel. The unjust way in which my upbringing went: My whole life I have been lied to by her, and yet it is I who got punished when I lied to her and disobeyed her. The paintings, this innate talent of mine, those kept me somewhat sane. And Martynn knew that about me. I think that is why he gave me this wonderful, beautiful quill on that durnal... He wants me sane. At least I hope that's the reason. I have no other explanation.

Every time he looked at my paintings, he got struck by how detailed and unusual they are. He used to say they are a terrific piece of artwork. Which is why I keep most of them hidden... or so, I thought. I cannot really hide anything... too many spies. The moment I found out about the odious gullinfern spying on me, was when and why I first considered having one of my own.

Two reasons I love to paint so much. The first being that I have always done it since I was old enough to crawl. It seemed to calm me, even in those unheeding times, when the only things which mattered to me were Toyol and her warm hugs and sweet cakes. It was somehow exotic, putting on parchment my thoughts and as I started to grow older, it felt good to put everything that was topsy-turvy into sight. As if, watching my misfortunes come to life on parchment was going to help me feel better. It did not. Actually, it was counterproductive: because I would paint myself being lifted off the ground and it was a pretty terrifying sight and painful. I used to illustrate the way Godmother treated me; never giving herself away and it felt demeaning. I painted one time, a scene of her summoning the leather strap she used to hit me with, the way it appeared aloft in between us, and how she would make me grab it by the handle and give it back to her, and the way I had to bend over the back of this same chair I am sitting in or the surface of the desk in her office. That was the norm! There was that time she made me bend over a high-stool in the kitchen and gave me a beating with Toyol present, who promised and I am certain she did, to close her eyes during the act. And those other time when she used other stuff to hit me with, on my knuckles, or my palms or.... ah! I refuse to talk about that any further!

In those moments all I wanted was to snuff out from existence. She was pretty aggressive, always so aloof, managing to keep herself insensitive and noncommittal. My intentions had been that of drawing her in comical ways, to mock her, trying in vain to put on a wry smile. I never managed to get to that point. Tears would roll down, and I had to stop altogether, it was too humiliating. I had shown the paintings to Toyol, and she made me realise they were only making me sad and were of no help whatsoever! So I burnt them in the furnace...

That is why I resorted to something happier in future times. I painted my dreams. What I longed for. That gave me something to look forward to. And made me, in some way, feel less of a recluse.

Not that painting managed to help empty my mind, but it was of help, to relieve the overflow. Also helped, on most occasions to keep my Seher at bay, and thus saved me some beatings.

The second reason is that I was too scared, and at times, too coy to talk with Martynn or Toyol about my feelings. Well, strictly speaking, I had no one else to talk to. Not only could not I converse properly with Martynn - because of the above-mentioned reasons — but given that his visits were so rare and didn't last long, we preferred to use them to have some fun and play games. My feelings became something that was better left unsaid, at times. Albeit, we talked about them, briefly, during our rides, around the castle grounds. I found that I could not confide properly with anyone else, that is why parchment and paintings, ink and quills became my place-to-go to let it all out.

That brings me back to the quill gifting anecdote - It took Martynn a long time to console me and make me feel at ease with myself and had he not gifted me this quill, I probably would have never recovered from that oddity - I was so perplexed about the lack of scolding!

He said he made it especially for me, keeping in mind my many complaints, that the coloured ink-pots I previously used in my drawings were never enough, or weren't vibrant enough to finish the paintings the way I wanted them. I just had to dip this fantastic quill in whatever liquid I had at hand (even saliva he had said), and voilà — the job was done. The colours would be endless, and as vibrant as I wished them to be. I think about the colour, see like now, I'm angry because I realized how oppressed my life is, and how Godmother always managed to have her way with me. So, I'm thinking black …

void... onyx. See the black drops oozing from the quill ... that is how it works. How all Seher works.

'It all depends on how you think,' Martynn explained in detail and frequently. Everything around us is about thinking ... your point of view, your intentions and most of all your most inner emotions. We are made of emotions, us Shahhar are. Or well, us Seher-wielders, we go by so many titles. Perhaps even this journal is Seherial - oh please, be such. I cannot know until I find a way to make it work.

That was the reason he invited himself to dinner at that time because he was impatient to see the quill at work in my hands. I did a little painting for him then, as a thank you token. I drew his gullinfern and gifted him the painting. He left immediately after helping me finish the missing academics, I had lied about. I cried myself to sleep, as I had done almost every sleeping-hin (time) after that episode.

After Godmother had finished, I would trudge miserably to the lavatory and look at the scars left on my bottom, crying and lamenting on how would I be able to sit to finish my academics. I was not permitted to finish them anywhere else if not sitting on my desk chair. Painful moments, which stung more than a thousand and one needles all at once.

She's so evil, Godmother is a cruel personage, I used to think so, or perhaps she really is. It's confusing, I never know how to talk to her, about her even. She is self-possessed, that she sure is if that is the word to use, uncertain about the spelling. Am no good with words. There was this one time when I had spent a durnal asking her, pleading with her to let me outside, for a little while, I would say. Just some fresh air, let me go somewhere new, somewhere I never went to. Let me go to the village, you can accompany me. I would insist. Nothing, she would not budge. In the end, after a dinner of tasty lampi-fish fried in Makkja-fruit oil, she said to me 'be well-behaved the following durnal, and turn in your academics in the proper manner and work hard on them, and the durnal after that you will be free to do what you want.' I cannot, not in a million aniums describe the sensation of that moment. I could not believe my ears... I stared for some time, quite a long time, I did. I managed to come back to my senses when I felt a cold hand pull at my earlobe and a scolding, 'do not be so fussy,' she said. 'You will have to work for your reward.' I jumped out of my seat as soon as she let go of my earlobe, I started jumping around the room, until I bumped into some invisible barrier which Godmother had conjured, 'Visblelehajt', now I know the spell. And if she had conjured it aloud at that moment I do not know. 'Dinner is over, Ewl, to bed with you,' she said then, while I was rubbing my nose which had hit the barrier. I did not know what to think. I know that I spent many many many, much time talking about it to Toyol, and she was all the time, doing her best to calm me. She told me not to think too much about it, that at the end it might turn out to be a disappointment, but at that moment in time, I did not want to believe her. I had a quarrel with her. I told her I wanted to believe it was true. This went on for the following durnal at breakfast, because after breakfast I did not want to talk about it any longer. The thought of having a durnal all to myself lingered inside me all that time until it was time to give Godmother the finished academic work. I presented it to her with a beating heart and almost no breath at all. I had prepared for that durnal, I wore my best frock, and with some help from Toyol, whom I had forgiven, my hair was perfectly coiffed. While proffering my work I started to become a tad apprehensive, knowing, having the sensation that perhaps Toyol was right on insisting that I might be disappointed at the outcome of this splendid idea of having a durnal to go down to the village and meet Lenom, a grown-up Lenom. Guess what, dear journal. Toyol was right!

Tears are flowing down my

cheeks, as I am prone on my bed writing on you with Martynn's quill. The remembrance of that durnal is too much for me to hold inside. She said, Godmother did, after perusing my work that it was fine and I could go play outside, have my free durnal. Oh, the happiness, the joy, the beating of my heart. I rushed to the kitchen to give the news to Toyol, she felt happy for a moment, I could sense that in her. A bitter-sweet moment, as then she sent 'be careful, Ewl, this might not be what you think". I ignored her, of course. How dare she, doubt this marvellous thing even now that is was happening? So I ran, one sprint from the kitchen door to the main gate, giddiness overflowing my body. I could feel my feet starting to levitate, but sadly, still until this very durnal, I do not know how to levitate all by myself. At that moment it was a lucky attribute that I could not, 'cause one touch of seher coming from me would mean a beating and bye-bye freedom. I came to the gate, and looked up at the unsleeping effigies, I told them to open the gate, as I had seen Godmother do on many occasions, but nothing happened. I waited and asked the effigies again, more politely this time, I said please. Nothing happened, the gate stayed closed. A rush of cold and warmth started to form inside me, I think it was anger or betrayal. I felt it then, Godmother's lie, she was not going to let me out. And I remembered Lenom, he had come from the back door that first time, I rushed there, my hopes rising again, I looked up at scorching Xemxa, she was there, warming Miragasia with her rays. Everything was, as usual, calm. No noise, and a whiff of pepper coming from the kitchen. I looked backwards, Toyol was at the window, looking at me. 'Go try the back gate,' she sent. 'I am here ready to lend a shoulder if need be.' So I went, I simply went, blinded by the fact that it might turn out to be right. Though it wasn't. The unsleeping effigies at the back-gate were uncooperative also. It was not going the way I dreamt it. I went back to the kitchen, with a broken heart. Silently I sat on the high stool and stared at the window. My brain blanked. A rush of something which made me want to break my head and everything around me filled my body in one instant. 'Fawra', that's the spell, I said. 'Do not do this, please,' Toyol sent. I did not care, I jumped down the stool and with one loud bang I rushed towards Godmother's study-chamber. She had heard me come, it seems, as she was waiting for me in the centre of the entrance hall. Stoic, self-possessed she stood, waiting... 'You are cruel,' I yelled, without thinking. 'You lied to me! A slap hit me hard on my left cheek. I stood there, unyielding. She told me to stop yelling, and I had no right to act in this foolish mannerism, and without knowing how I found myself back in my chamber, with the door locked. She was there, too. Standing as straight as earlier with a threat, that she would blister my behind if I were not calm. For some unknown reason, I calmed down. I was not scared of a blistered behind, I was used to that. Perhaps, I was. I still was, yes. Though, I was more afraid that the promised diurnal of freedom would not happen. It did, but not in the way I had thought. Godmother starting explaining to me, in a calm tone that a diurnal of freedom for me would never mean I would go to the village, but it simply meant that for the diurnal the rules of the castle hold will not apply. I could have meals what time I wanted and I did not have to study. I could go as far as the fields, and go to bed what time I wanted, as long as I stayed within the castle-grounds, I had to abide, no matter what. Yelling and revenge will be of no help. I found myself saying that Toyol was right,

I should have listened. I cried alone, on this very bed. Cried so much that I regurgitated. Cried at the fact that I was not going to see Lenom any time soon. Toyol came to clean the mess and bring me a hot beverage, with some biscuits she had made for the occasion. I had been crying over an illustration I had made of Lenom, how I imagined he would be as a grown Melitasian. I studied their anatomy in various books. I had made the painting with the intention of gifting it to him once we met at the village that fateful diurnal. It did not happen, it did not go the way I planned.

This is the illustration, for some reason (certainly by seher) stamped itself on the next page, as soon as I started writing about it... Go figure!

Nevertheless the diurnal turned out to be a fun one. I was still allowed outside, despite my earlier mal-disposition, as Godmother put it. She said, that with how I comported myself she should have given me a beating and locked me in. Though, she added that a word given is a done deed, so she had to keep to hers. Thusly she let me have my durnal-of-freedom.

I spent the durnal preparing meals with Toyol and tending the hmejels. In the end, I wanted to have dinner with Toyol, but Godmother decided that I was going to have dinner with her, as she said the diurnal was almost over and I had to do what she said. I told her that I prefered to go to bed with a blistered behind and have dinner with Toyol. My despondent behaviour, as she put it, was going to be of no use, and I had to do what she said. Even because Toyol suggested I should be obedient and perhaps Godmother would permit me another diurnal such as this.

I cried all the way back to my chamber after dinner. I had some time left to spend in freedom before going to bed. So, I decided to make another painting. I went back down to the kitchen to proffer my gift to Toyol. It was a painting of us, having dinner together. I could see tears forming in Toyol. 'It is striking,' she sent. 'Do you like it. So?' I asked aloud. 'It's perfect,' she sent. I went to bed, holding Lenom's image close to my heart. I still have that painting, neatly rolled in the first drawer of my desk. One durnal, sometime, sometime, perhaps... I will show it to him.

DIURNAL IIIII

Perhaps. Perhaps, something a little more formal.

My name is Ewliena.

Nothing.

Come on I am trying to be polite...

Frustrating parchment, you are!

Toyol once told me that 'my name

is' is probably better to say than 'I am'; because there is more to who we are than just our name.

Perhaps, I should draw on you... let's see.

There! A drawing of me sitting astride Makkja... with my dreams and hopes drawn in the background.

Do you like it, diary?

Journal?

Blank parchment! Useless blank

parchment!

Ew-lie-na!

Bah, what's in a name anyway?

Well, there is in mine: the word 'in' is in my name...

There's lie in it. Godmother says I'm a liar, and, honestly, I am one... and I am apparently always on fire. I am a living fire.

Law ... not that, according to Godmother, I have not much

respect for the law ...

Nail... spelt backwards is Lian ... Lian can be a good name.

Win... yeah, win what?

New also--there's new in it. I am new... my name means new, or first, or alone, or at the beginning. Or all of them amalgamated; I am something new.

Ewl – They call me that for short, I am of the conviction that in Melitasian it means 'beginning', but I'm not a 100% sure.

Anew is also in there.

Hybrid... that is not in it, but I am one. Miscegenation neither is in it. I heard Godmother use that word many times, though. I never asked what it meant, or why was she so firmly stubborn about the word.

Lena; that would've been a good name, too. Or lane, a lane of ... narrow-minded, I might be... who knows!

Lean... Leena... I am lean, too. My name might be all there is to me after all. I'm a ray of sunshine (and so apparently I can become as bright and as scorching as Xemxa), freedom and, well, a tree of sorts... I've never seen a palm tree. Martynn has told me about them. I have an illustration of myself showing my hair transform into tree-branches. It was a dream I had and I wanted to remember it...

Alina... why isn't my name Alina or Aline? Or, something completely different!

Line--I cannot think straight... my line of thought is inexistent. I never think one thought at a time!

I give up!

Ail... I'm a constant disappointment to Dame Vellja, that must ail her, or not? She certainly ails me...

I sprawled on my bed, prone,

groaning and moaning ... twisted to one side and shut my eyes. Fighting the strong urge to hurl the journal against the wall. I proceeded to take a long bath, drained down the cup of milk which Toyol had brought me earlier, devoured the sugar-coated flower-shaped biscuit, I helped her bake (my favourite snack). Had another bath, looked out of the eastward window, gave a long sigh and settled comfortably, back against the window-frame, on the window seat, journal on lap writing... again.

The durnal I transformed into a Monster of Fire:

I can't remember much after I fainted in Martynn's arm. I don't know how much time passed. What I do remember clearly is Godmother pulling at my hair so tightly that I had a hard time standing straight, and yet I could not even voice my suffering, she caught me unawares - the pain it seemed had abandoned me, and my senses went dormant. Godmother had always been angry at me, at times even furious, I dare say since the very first diurnal she brought me to the castle. I don't know if, by any chance, she felt some love for me. She is unfathomable to me, and she did not exhibit any other emotions other than anger and most extreme severity. Petulant she used to call me, (she still does) and those very few moments she used to give me permission to go out in the garden, she used to do with the same severity. But, I used to be so jolly about those moments, that I would not even give her the time to finish her sentence, that I would be already out and climbing Makkja. And when she called me back inside, I used to do so with acquiescence.

She had also been extremely careful at hiding her anger by suppressing it so tightly that at times it was almost as if it had never been there. Those few moments of respite, were for me the only times I could truly feel the burden of living. It was like the respite was a reminder that I will never be completely liberated. Those were the moments I spent with Toyol working on our communication skills, and in those times, most of the time, I wished to be Seherless.

Dame Vellja manifested some of her furies when she clouted me with that leather strap or the leather belt - that dreaded strap; every time I saw it aloft - it used to appear in between us, right before my eyes, the instant she summoned it, mocking me, asking me to await the fate it was going to impose on me, there floating just at eye level - my body hair would stand on end, and my face would turn as crimson as my curls, and the blows would leave me inert for three or four subsequent durnals. Apart from the considerable pain, I would feel inept. I wanted to kill myself so badly; and, I tried many times. Nothing seemed to work, not even a knife in the gut: it would crumble to pieces in my hand, every single time the point touched me. It only added to my feeling of ineptitude.

That leather strap made my buttocks throb in anticipation ever time, and my interns turn cold — quite contrary to my skin which, by the third blow would already be completely red-hot. Why did I never listen to Toyol's advice? I should have listened. She always told me that I should do what I was told. That would lessen the anger of Dame Vellià. But did I ever even try to listen? I recall that at times I did... but those times lasted a few moments. Then my petulance would kick in, and I would be in trouble again. Chiding and cursing myself, crying in bed, hugging a pillow. At times talking to it as though it were my crony; Blulaksa I called it. I don't know how or why; the name just came to me one durnal.

That strap: strips of thick brown, heavy, leather, sewn together, about two feet long and three inches wide, which had made me stare at it with an open mouth (agape if you may) the first time I saw it. I believe I was about nine or ten. I had used my Seher to light up a fire in the garden. All I wanted to do that time, was use smoke signals, to attract someone's attention. I had been sure someone down from the village would see them, understand and come save me. The only attraction it attracted was that of Dame Vellià...

But when things got so bad, then she summoned Eluvia. When that happened no matter how hard I pulled, I could not pull free from Eluvia's massive hands. I would brace myself, rest my face down on the cloth scrap that was her frock, groaning my anger and misery, my head resting on her hard belly choking on my own saliva. The first stroke always struck me by surprise, no matter how prepared I was. It would make me jump out of my skin and scream my interns away...

It was like she was letting her anger get the best of her that time, she simply couldn't repress it any longer, and she slapped me so hard that when my head touched the floor, I started to bleed from head and mouth. Still, I could not scream, nor let out the slightest outcry. Then I was being apathetically dragged by the hair towards her office, and there I was being bent down over the wooden desk, and a while later I was being beaten mercilessly - what with, I don't know. Still, nothing came out of my mouth and neither from hers. Four, five times, tenfold that, my brain felt like it was being split to pieces with every blow. She was an expert at beating me with perfect aim until but an inch of my breath, using the strap with extreme precision always on the same spot. Usually, by the tenth stroke, I would be screaming and frothing saliva, kicking furiously. That time I was intent in keeping it all in no matter how much she came whipping down. I did not budge. And praised myself for my braveness until I lost track of the beating...

With a sudden jerk, my head got

lifted up again, and I heard the words 'look up' - so I did. There was an image clearly formed in front of me; it had been there by a sort of distorted imaginary created by Seher. I could see the village as clear as if I were there, but I wasn't.

I know it was the village where Lenom resided, the one I would watch from the bell tower or when I was on top on Makkja. I recognized the thatched colourful roofs, I knew them by heart, with my eyes closed tightly I could still be able to describe them thoroughly. My beloved village on fire. Meltisians panicking and screaming as they tried to suppress the fires, pieces of splintering ambers fighting a way back to life. Feet stepping on broken pieces of wood. At that moment a strange thought came to me: what was taking all my attention: the fire inflicted and suffusing my behind and thighs in one big raw bruise or the smoke and flames burning the village down to ashes? Everything was so contorted. I might have gotten a glimpse of him, Lenom, holding a bucket full of water, in his right hand and gesturing with his left. Watching as the roaring fire engulfed a building, before ripping savagely through. All his possessions were gone.

Tendrils of smoke seemed to be calling my name in desperation. The entire village burned, the fires grew rapidly, with no intention to cease, red and orange sparks flew in front of my eyes. Screams of Melitasians echoed through my ears, there to stay. If there was something I knew perfectly well, inside out, was Fire. I willed it to stop hurting them.

A full blow hit me again, which made me give up my silence with a loud scream, I could feel the walls vibrate. Godmother said: 'you might not realise it, yet, but you're doing this to them, you're burning us up.' Then another incensed blow hit my thighs. 'No,' I stated firmly, 'no it cannot be!'

'Use your mindcommunication, look inside your head, you'll see!' Another intensified blow made me startle and kick my legs in frustration, and then ... a pang! A spiritual one! Guilt hit me as I realised that she was right.

I could not feel anything anymore, it was like my body, my

senses and everything else around me had melted into a puddle of blood and fire. If, as Godmother puts it the punishment should fit the crime then she was doing a great job at that.

Then I heard Godmother talk again, 'this is what you get if you keep this up. In lieu of burning us to death, you will be the one burnt. These plights of yours need to be stopped; they are unsuccessful anyway! Are you unable to understand that none of us can do anything?' And the severe chiding went on in this way, she let out her anger in full this time punctuating every word with a heavy blow. She blamed me and my family for the destruction of Miragasia. She stated we are a selfish bunch and with our selfishness, we destroyed everything that was once good and beautiful. I could not get myself to believe how biased she was against me and my entire kin. She was saying out loud, that the fire was coming from me and I was the one who was making the Melitisians suffer in that way. My ways were arcane, selfish and cruel. Like the rest of my kin was. She said I destroyed Eluvia to save my skin, and with that, I could feel the biggest physical pain of it all, as the whatever it was hit and hit mercilessly, with an onslaught of pain. And yet, I could not cry. I was dry from the inside.

DIURNAL IIIIII

Imagine this: being hit by someone twice your size - someone who you would love – imagine the first couple of times when you wouldn't know when it would stop or if the one you trusted so much was going to kill you! It damages you for a long time. And as time goes by, as you start to get older, you still have the same feelings.

Now, that is decuple worse when you get the same thing by some monster tenfold your size. Eluvia. It's sad, and painful inside and out. It's like your bones are being broken and fixed only to be broken again until you faint. What I recall the most, is the split second before the fainting occurs, the discomfort I experience between waking or sleeping trying to think of something to say apart from 'I'm sorry, please stop.' And the unbearable revelation, that it never stops ... the pain holds on.

Debilitated and inert I fell on the floor. 'Why,' I said heaving with the effort. 'Why are you doing this?'

No reply. Then someone put me in bed again and I slept. Dreaming of the dark. I only saw the darkness that once, when I ran away and I met Abyshaelle, my grandfather and Nebur for the first time in my life. I love the dark,

I hanker for it to come. I do not know what happened to Abyshaelle. I wish to know.

Perhaps that is why I love to sleep so much, cause when I close my eyes the light is gone. The seher which resides in me, I am ashamed to say it that of destruction, whilst I am fully heartedly certain that my parents thrived in seher of creation.

I want to change it all! I want to change the way life is!

An ink-splotch reverberated

and so did Miragasia

Note from the author

This is a journal which came in the hands of Ewliena one day when she was trudging around the castle she lives in. The entire tale of how this came to be is written in The Upbringing, as are all descriptions of the creatures and other characters mentioned within.

May the seher last forever.

The Covers of Book One

Available on Amazon Paperback and e-book

Printed in Great Britain
by Amazon